Why Can't I Play?

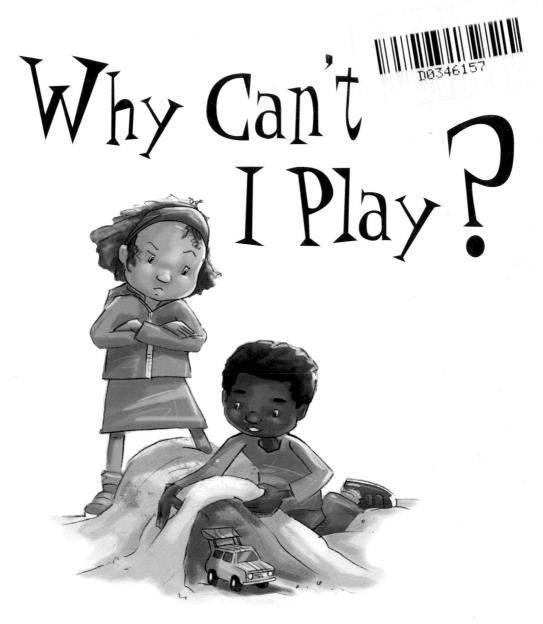

by Elizabeth Hawkins
Illustrated by Bill Bolton

WHY CAN'T I PLAY
TAMARIND BOOKS 978 1 848 53016 4

Published in Great Britain by Tamarind Books,
a division of Random House Children's Books
A Random House Group Company

This edition published 2010

1 3 5 7 9 10 8 6 4 2

TAMARIND BOOKS
61–63 Uxbridge Road, London, W5 5SA

www.**tamarindbooks**.co.uk
www.**kids**at**randomhouse**.co.uk
www.**rbooks**.co.uk

Addresses for companies within The Random House Group Limited can be found at:
www.randomhouse.co.uk/offices.htm

THE RANDOM HOUSE GROUP Limited Reg. No. 954009

A CIP catalogue record for this book is available from the British Library.

Printed and bound in China

To Lauren
E.H.

To Ben and Amy
B.B.

The summer holidays had come and every day
Thomas went to play in the sandpit in the park.
Grandpa took him and he met his friends.

They made tunnels for their cars and
built castles for their soldiers.
They drew strange shapes and pictures
with their fingers in the sand.

One day when Thomas and his friends played in the sandpit, a new girl came.

She stood close by them,
much too close for such a large sandpit.

Down she sat,
blocking the entrance to their tunnel.
"Get out of the way!" said Thomas.
"It's not your sandpit," said the girl.
"I can do what I want."

"But we are playing here," said Thomas.
"Go away. Play somewhere else."
"I don't want to. I'm staying right here," said the girl.
"I have lots of sand at home... enough for a desert,
and it's so hot it frazzles up boys like you."

The next day the new girl jumped
into the sandpit again.

Thomas and his friends stayed
away from her, but the girl followed them.
Thomas drew a picture with his spade in the sand.
"What's that?" said the girl.
"A spotted sand monster," said Thomas.
"It's a silly squiggle," said the girl.
She drew zig-zag patterns all over the monster.

"You spoiled my spotted sand monster!" yelled Thomas. "Why don't you stay at home and draw in your desert? We don't want you here."

"I can't," said the girl.
"We took the sand away,
dug a hole and filled it with water."
"Why?" asked Thomas.
"To make a lake. We put crocodiles in it
that eat boys like you."

On the third day, Thomas and his friends
were building a huge sand castle
when the new girl arrived.

She skipped round and round
until the towers crumbled.
"You should have packed the sand down harder
in your buckets," said the new girl.

"You spoiled our castle!" said Thomas angrily.
"Go away and feed your crocodiles."
"Those towers were tiny," said the girl.

"You should see the towers at our house.
We have a tower that goes up to the sky.
If boys like you don't get frazzled in the desert
and don't get eaten by crocodiles,
we can lock you up in the tallest tower."

On the fourth day Thomas and his friends pretended not to see the new girl. She sat by herself on the sandpit wall.

The new girl's mother came over.
"It's Becca's birthday," she said.
"Would you all like to come for tea?"
She gave an invitation each to Thomas and his friends.

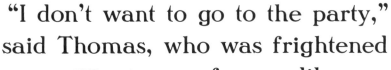

"I don't want to go to the party," said Thomas, who was frightened of crocodiles.

"I get sun burned in deserts," said the girl with red hair.

"I don't want to get locked up," said the smallest boy.

"A birthday tea... how nice, thank you!" said the children's parents.

So the children went.

There was no desert so they played in the heap
of sand the builders had left.

They searched the pond for crocodiles but there were only tadpoles and they didn't bite.

They played with the castle the new girl's father had made for her birthday.

There was a feast of crisps and hamburgers and drinks.
There were cup cakes and crunchy biscuits and
ice cream and there was the stickiest,
finger-licking chocolate cake that Thomas and
his friends had ever tasted.

Becca blew out the birthday candles.
"Wish!" the children shouted.
"I wish... I wish I could play with you in the park."

The next day Thomas met Becca at the sandpit.
"Please can I play with you?" asked Becca.
"Of course," said Thomas. "You only had to ask!"

OTHER TAMARIND TITLES

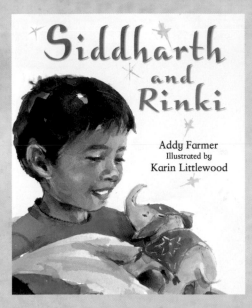

Siddharth and Rinki
A story about a lost toy, making friends
and getting used to a new life.

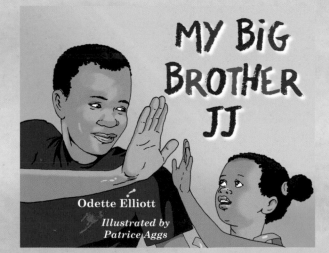

Big Eyes, Scary Voice
An amazing twilight adventure with evocative
illustrations, perfect for bedtime reading.

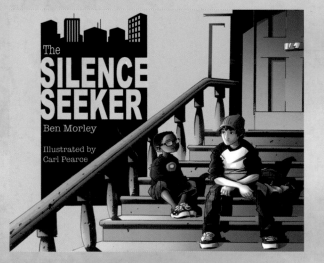

The Silence Seeker
Joe tries to make friends with a mysterious new
neighbour - a 'silence seeker' - in this haunting
and lyrical perspective on immigration.

My Big Brother JJ
An affectionate portrayal of family life,
with an older brother looking after his little
sister while Mum is at work.

FOR READERS OF *Why Can't I Play?*

Danny's Adventure Bus
North American Animals
South African Animals
Caribbean Animals
The Night the Lights Went Out
All My Friends
A Safe Place
Choices, Choices...
What Will I Be?
Dave and the Tooth Fairy
Time for Bed
Time to Get Up
Giant Hiccups
Are We There Yet?
Mum's Late

BOOKS FOR WHEN THEY GET A LITTLE OLDER
Amina and the Shell
The Dragon Kite
Princess Katrina and the Hair Charmer
The Feather
Marty Monster
Starlight
Boots for a Bridesmaid
Yohance and the Dinosaurs